Ellen Ochoa:
First Hispanic Woman Astronaut

Maritza Romero

The Rosen Publishing Group's
PowerKids Press™
New York

Published in 1997 by The Rosen Publishing Group, Inc.
29 East 21st Street, New York, NY 10010

First Edition

Book Design: Danielle Primiceri

Photo Credits: Cover, pp. 4, 7, 11, 16 (inset), 19 (all photos) © Gamma Liaison; all other photos © AP/Wide World Photos.

Romero, Maritza.
    Ellen Ochoa : the first Hispanic woman astronaut / Maritza Romero.
        p.   cm. — (Great Hispanics of Our Time)
    Summary: Profiles the life of the first Hispanic woman to become an astronaut including information about her childhood, education, and career with NASA.
    ISBN 0-8239-5087-5
    1. Ochoa, Ellen—Juvenile literature. 2. Woman astronauts—United States—Biography—Juvenile literature. 3. Hispanic Americans in the professions—Juvenile literature. 4. Hispanic American women—Biography—Juvenile literature. [1.Ochoa, Ellen. 2. Women astronauts. 3. Hispanic Americans—Biography. 4. Women—Biography.] I. Title. II. Series.
    TL789.85.O25R66 1997
    629.45'0092—dc21   97-11546
                                                                                                      CIP
                                                                                                      AC

Manufactured in the United States of America

Contents

A Good Example

Ellen Ochoa was born on May 10, 1958 in Los Angeles, California. She is half Mexican, and is proud of her Hispanic heritage.

Ellen's mother, Rosanne, taught her five children that a good education could help them to be anything they wanted. And Rosanne set a good example. She took college classes for 23 years and earned three **degrees** (dih-GREEZ). Today, she is a **journalist** (JER-nul-ist) for a newspaper called the *San Diego Union Tribune*. From her mother, Ellen learned that she could be anything she wanted, even an **astronaut** (AS-tro-not).

◀ Ellen Ochoa learned about hard work from her mother. Hard work helped her to become an astronaut.

Favorite Subjects

Ellen loved school and she was not afraid to work hard. Her favorite subjects were math and music, but she did well in all of her classes. She also loved to read. One of the books she liked most was *A Wrinkle in Time*, a book about a girl who travels through time. Ellen especially liked the fifth grade. During that year, the teacher split the class into two groups. Each group pretended to be a country. Ellen liked learning about other countries.

Ellen brought her love of learning to every job that she had. ▶

A Top Performer

When Ellen was thirteen, she won the San Diego spelling bee. She was named "outstanding seventh and eighth grade student." By the time Ellen was in high school, she was known for being an excellent student. Ellen could also play the flute very well. She was a top performer in her high school. She was so good that she was asked to play with the Civic Youth Orchestra in San Diego. When Ellen graduated, she had the highest grades of anyone in her class.

◀ Ellen had to be the best to become an astronaut.

Changing Her Mind

Ellen was the top math student in high school, but no one told her how a person, especially a woman, could get a job using math. She went to San Diego State University in 1975. There, she decided she would study either music or business. But she changed her mind five times. No matter what she did, she kept coming back to math. She knew that there had to be something she could do with her love of math.

When Ellen was young, some people didn't think that women could do jobs that involved math or science. But as an astronaut, Ellen proved that she, and other women, could work in those fields. ▶

The Right Decision

Ellen decided to talk to her **physics** (FIZ-iks) and her **engineering** (en-jin-EER-ing) professors. She hoped they could help her decide what she should do. Her engineering professor wrongly told her that engineering was too hard for a girl. But her physics professor said she would enjoy physics. She took two more physics classes and decided that her physics professor was right. Ellen graduated from San Diego State University in 1980 with a degree in physics.

◀ Ellen was glad she followed the advice of her physics professor. It helped her find a job that she loved.

Ellen the Inventor

After earning her physics degree, Ellen decided to try engineering. And in 1985, she earned a second degree, this one in electrical engineering. She started working at Sandia National Laboratories and became an **inventor** (in-VEN-ter). With another engineer, she invented two different ways to work with **optics** (OP-tiks). She began speaking and writing about her work so others could learn about it. But she still made time to play her flute. She even won an award for her performance with the Stanford Symphony Orchestra.

Ellen used her knowledge of optics in space. This is a picture ▶ of Ellen explaining her job while she was in space.

A Good Choice

Ellen did not always know she would be an astronaut. But when some friends started talking about it, it sounded right for her. She found out what was needed to become a part of the **NASA** (NA-suh) space program. Ellen's study of math and engineering and even her love of music made her a good choice. In 1987, she became one of the top 100 people considered for the program.

◀ Once Ellen learned about NASA's space program, she knew that she wanted to be an astronaut.

Learning to Be an Astronaut

While she waited to hear if she was accepted by NASA, Ellen went to work for a NASA **research** (ree-SERCH) center. There she was in charge of a research team that studied ways optics could be used. Ellen also took up a new hobby. She learned how to fly an airplane, and got her private pilot's license.

In January 1990, NASA chose Ellen for their astronaut program. She and her new husband, Coe Fulmer Miles, moved to Houston, Texas, where the space program is located. It was time for her to learn how to be an astronaut.

It takes a lot of training to become an astronaut. ▶

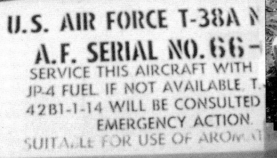

U.S. AIR FORCE T-38A N
A.F. SERIAL NO. 66-
SERVICE THIS AIRCRAFT WITH
JP-4 FUEL IF NOT AVAILABLE. T.
42B1-1-14 WILL BE CONSULTED
EMERGENCY ACTION.
SUITABLE FOR USE OF AROM

Heading for Space

On April 8, 1993, Ellen became the first Hispanic woman to fly into space. She and four male astronauts were aboard the **space shuttle** (SPAYS SHUT-tul) *Discovery*. This space mission studied the sun. Ellen's special job was to use a **robotic** (roh-BOT-ik) arm to send into space and then catch a small, 2,800-pound **satellite** (SA-tel-yt) called *Spartan*. The *Spartan* helped the astronauts learn more about the sun. On November 3, 1994, Ellen made a second flight into space on the space shuttle *Atlantis*.

◀ Ellen's first trip into space was in the space shuttle *Discovery*.

A Lucky Job

Today, Ellen speaks to students about her job as an astronaut. She tells them that she didn't always know what kind of job she would do. But she learned that there are a lot of jobs to choose from.

Ellen tells kids that if they follow their dreams, study hard, and don't give up, they can be whatever they want to be.

Being the first Hispanic woman astronaut has meant a lot to Ellen. She is a hero to kids, especially girls, who are interested in math, science, or becoming astronauts.

Glossary

astronaut (AS-tro-not) A person who travels into space.

degree (dih-GREE) Something a person gets when they complete college studies.

engineering (en-jin-EER-ing) The study of how to design and build things.

inventor (in-VEN-ter) A person who makes something new.

journalist (JER-nul-ist) A person who writes and reports stories about real life for newspapers, magazines, or television shows.

NASA (NA-suh) The National Aeronautics and Space Administration. It is the place where people study outer space and train to be astronauts.

optics (OP-tiks) A science that studies the way people see.

physics (FIZ-iks) The study of the way things move.

research (ree-SERCH) The careful study of something to find out more information.

robot (ROH-bot) A machine that completes difficult tasks.

satellite (SA-tel-yt) Something that can fly on its own in space to help astronauts get more information.

space shuttle (SPAYS SHUT-tul) Spacecraft that carries people and equipment between space and Earth.

Index